British Library Cataloguing in Publication Data

Newman, Nanette
  Pigalev.
  I. Title   II. Smith, Lesley
  823'.914 [J]   PZ7

  ISBN 0-340-33855-5

Text copyright © 1985 Bryan Forbes Ltd
Illustrations copyright © 1985 Hodder and Stoughton Ltd
First published 1985

Published by Hodder and Stoughton Children's Books,
a division of Hodder and Stoughton Ltd,
Mill Road, Dunton Green, Sevenoaks, Kent TN13 2YJ

Printed in Great Britain by Cambus Litho, East Kilbride

Pigalev

Nanette Newman

Illustrations by Lesley Smith

HODDER AND STOUGHTON
LONDON SYDNEY AUCKLAND TORONTO

To come out of your Mummy's tummy, to lie in the straw, looking up at the stars on a warm June night, is a very pleasant way to take your first look at the world. The moment Mrs. Pig looked at the three squealing babies, she loved them. She thought they were the most beautiful piglets she'd ever seen. They weren't, of course, but she thought they were.

She took the greatest care of them.
Fed them till their pink tummies
were full and nuzzled them with her
snout.
They grew quite quickly, became
cheeky and naughty, disobeyed their
Mother from time to time, were
always sorry and were always loved.

Mrs. Pig chose names that went well with Pig. James and Gerald for the boys, and Lucinda for the girl. "Lucinda Pig," she would say softly to herself.

"Oh what a pretty girl you are." She wasn't pretty at all really, but as long as someone *thought* she was, what did it matter.

Soon they were old enough to go to school.

If you thought pigs didn't go to school, you'd be wrong. It may not be your type of school, but then you'd hardly expect that, would you?

Anyway, they went to school and quite soon they started to think about what they would be when they grew up.

Both the boys chose quite sensible things to want to be, but much to everyone's amazement Lucinda announced that she wanted to be a ballet dancer. Not just any ballet dancer – but the *best ballet dancer in the world.*

You are probably thinking that it's impossible for a pig to become a dancer, even perhaps to dance at all; well, you'd be wrong – because nothing is impossible and Mrs. Pig knew that as well as anyone.

"If you want to become a dancer – then a dancer you'll become," she said to Lucinda. Lucinda smirked and poked out her tongue at her brothers for sniggering at her.

Her Mother bought her red ballet shoes, and a record of Swan Lake, and took her to ballet class every Friday.
You might think a pig would look silly in tights and a leotard and ballet shoes doing a Grande-Jeté.
Well you'd be right, of course, but it's rude to laugh at things like that.

After Lucinda had been dancing for a year she heard about an audition.
A ballet company needed a new leading ballerina and **"anyone interested should go to the theatre tomorrow at 10 o'clock."**
Lucinda arrived at half past nine, put on the ballet dress (made by Mrs. Pig specially) and sat in the wings watching the other dancers arrive. "Next please," she heard a voice say. "It's you," someone whispered. She walked out on to the stage. "Name?" asked the stage-manager.
"Pigalev" she said.

I know it's the first time you've heard that name, well – that's because it was the first time Lucinda had ever said it. She'd said it to herself lots of times, but never out loud.

**"Pigalev
the Greatest Ballet Dancer
in the world."**

"Start please," said a voice from the darkness. The music from Swan Lake began and so did Lucinda (I mean of course Pigalev).

One, two, three Grande–Jeté en tournant, one, two, three, Glissade (her little feet sped across the floor). Arabesque, two, three. Just as she was getting to the really fast bit the voice said, "That's enough. We'll let you know." Pigalev left the stage.

They had said *we'll let you know.* But they never did.

That night she was quite quiet – Mrs. Pig sent the boys off to bed earlier than usual and took her daughter on her knee.

For a while they sat – just looking into the fire. Then big tears fell out of Lucinda's eyes and on to Mrs. Pig's apron.

"I'm not going to be the greatest dancer in the world," she said between sobs. "I'm probably not even going to be a very good dancer at all."

Mrs. Pig kissed her and held her more tightly. "Now you listen carefully, Lucinda," she said. "Sometimes when we want something, very badly, and we don't get it, it seems as though it's the end of the world, but do you know, it isn't. Some people never even have the pleasure of *trying* to be the best dancer in the world. Just think of that. The most important thing is *never* to give up, but to keep on trying."

It was good advice. Lucinda did become a dancer, (no, not the best in the world) but she was certainly very good and Mrs. Pig was so proud of her when she saw

**"Pigalev
the Dancing Pig
in
Swan Lake,"**

that she almost cried.
Well almost, she was so busy applauding that there wasn't really any time for tears.